Science Fiction Romance

Hunting Camion

A Time Travel Futuristic Novella
by Raleigh Kincaid

Science Fiction Romance
Hunting Camion
A Time Travel Futuristic Novella
by Raleigh Kincaid
Published by Indie Artist Press
Eagle Mountain, Utah
www.indieartistpress.com
Second Paperback Edition
copyright © 2013-2015
All rights reserved.
ISBN-10: 1-62522-050-2
ISBN-13: 978-1-62522-050-9
May 2015

Praise for **Raleigh Kincaid**

Raleigh Kincaid is the pen name of award-winning and
Amazon Best Selling Author, Marjorie Jones.

For all the lovers who know that, when it comes to true love,

time and distance mean nothing at all.

CHAPTER ONE

Camion Drake straddled his motorcycle in the parking lot of his brother's biker bar in beautiful, downtown Pleasant, Utah. He sneered at the crumbling exterior before scanning the street in both directions.

What he saw didn't surprise him.

Nothing.

The main street had been boarded up when he'd left ten years ago, and it was boarded up today. Only now, the old merchants' signs that hung over the dirty sidewalks did so with one chain instead of two. The marquee over the town's sole movie theater blinked on and off, the title of the current movie misspelled.

A huge tumbleweed blew across the parking lot in front of him. Camion half-expected a coyote to howl in the distance.

What had possessed him to come back here? Didn't he have anything better to do with his time?

He pulled off the bandanna he'd used to keep his long hair out of his face and tied it to his handlebars. The sad truth was, he didn't. And his brother had promised him a job.

Good thing about brothers. With no town, no business, and no money, they could still offer each other jobs.

Camion dismounted his bike and made his way around four others parked in front of the dingy, blue metal door.

The inside of the bar looked exactly the same as the day he'd left for his BUD/S training. Dark. Ugly. Empty. Except for the four bikers who sat in the rear booth, no doubt planning their next bank robbery.

His brother, Constantine, glanced up from behind the bar. "Hey, you made it!"

"Wouldn't miss this for the world. You look swamped, man. How do you handle the stress?" Camion quirked an eyebrow and sat on a ragged stool at the end of the bar.

Con laughed. "Well, you know. Nerves of steel."

Camion leaned his elbows on the uneven counter and folded his fingers together. "What the hell am I doing here, bro?" He tried to sound lazy, like he didn't care.

"Somebody has to keep an eye on you for the next three years, right?"

"My parole officer said I need a job, not a babysitter." Camion glanced around the bar again for emphasis. "I don't see a job."

"You'll tend bar and throw people out when they need it. You'll keep the peace."

Camion glanced over his shoulder one more time, noting quietly that his brother wasn't real big on subtlety.

"It's Tuesday morning, for crissake. How busy do you expect things to be? Wait until Friday night when the miners' get their paychecks and this place will be standing room only."

"One can only hope," Camion answered, dryly. But at the least the mine was still open. Somebody was earning a living.

A thin stream of light on the bar beside him grew into a wide rectangle. Camion turned to the door and shaded his eyes. Several bodies, too small to be of any threat, blocked part of the sunlight blinding him. They stood in the doorway for several seconds before stepping inside and closing the door behind them.

Four women. Four maneaters, more likely.

The part of his anatomy most happy to be out of prison jumped in his jeans. He may not remember much from before his ten-year stint, but he remembered enough about this sort of thing. The hair. The makeup. The come-and-fuck-me heels and skirts. . .

These ladies were on the prowl.

He exchanged a quick glance with his brother, who shared an appreciative smirk. Suddenly remembering the shady-types in the back, he threw them a glare. They had already noticed the new arrivals, and one of them stood and adjusted his cock.

The women, moving like a well-oiled machine, approached the bar. Each of them took a stool, while three of them spun backwards and leaned their elbows on the torn, vinyl padding.

"Whiskey," the tall red-head purred. "Straight."

"Comin' right up," answered Con, reaching for the bottle. "Bro. You want to get to work?"

"My pleasure," he whispered, scooting off his own barstool and circling the bar.

"What'll it be, ladies?" he asked, putting on his best wild-west bartender attitude.

A brunette with shoulder-length curls glanced back at him over her almost-bare shoulder. With his height and the slight angle, he could see down her shirt. Her breasts were not too small, not too big. They'd fit in the palms of his hands nicely, he mused. The slight shadows of her black, strapless bra held them in place, but in his mind, he pictured them spilling free against his cheek. His cock hardened in his jeans.

Yeah. Ten years was a really, really long time.

"I'll have a double-shot with a Coors back."

"Jose Cuervo, I presume."

"Of course," the woman answered. "And lime."

"Only the best for a beautiful woman like you," Camion answered with a wink.

He turned around to grab the bottle of tequila gold from the shelf and when he turned back to the bar, the woman was facing him. Bright red lips pursed in a pouty grin, and she shifted her shoulders as though her legs were crossed and

6

bouncing one over the other. "So, what is there to do for fun in this town?" she asked, almost demure, but not quite.

He chuckled, admiring her act. "Oh, lots of things." *All of them illicit and best performed naked.*

"Care to show me?"

He almost choked. Instantly, he retraced the layout of the back offices in his mind. If nothing had changed since his father's death, there was a rather comfortable couch in the office, and a private storeroom behind the kitchen. "Show you what, exactly?"

"I'm bored. And lonely. I figured a big, strong man like you could show me a great way to occupy my time."

Con poured each of the other women a glass of beer. "Down boy," he whispered as he passed behind Camion. Louder, he asked the red-head with the whiskey, "What, exactly, brings you ladies to the middle of nowhere."

Red smiled. "You heard her. We're bored. We're just passing through, mind you, but this looked like a nice place to find a little . . . company."

It didn't seem possible, but judging from the looks the women threw not only to Camion and his brother, but the four men in the back, these gals were hornier than he was.

Camion leaned over the bar, fastened a level gaze on Tequila's bright, blue eyes, and grinned. "What's your game?"

She laughed. A genuine, full-bodied laugh that made his heart race. "I don't have a game, cowboy. I just want to get laid."

CHAPTER TWO

"Well, why didn't you say so?" Camion reached over the bar and took the woman's hand. She stood on the barstool, stepped onto the bar and fell into his arms. Slowly, he lowered her down the length of his chest, crotch, and legs, making sure she knew exactly how *up* for the event he really was. "Mind the bar, little brother. This might take a while."

"I'm Lynn, by the way," Tequila offered.

"I don't care," Camion answered with a wide smile.

Lynn's friends laughed and the red-head at the end waved. "Have fun, you two. Don't forget to take notes, Lynn."

Con rolled his eyes. "How is it that kind of thing always happens to him? I just don't get it. Everyone knows I'm better lookin'."

"Well, then. I guess, I'll just have to make it up to you," Red remarked, before downing the rest of her whiskey and leading Con around the end of the bar.

Camion ignored them and hurried Lynn into the back office. Dingy, covered with scattered papers and a collection of mismatched motorcycle parts, the place was anything but romantic. He shrugged when he opened the door and ushered the new love of his life into the room. "Sorry about the mess. We weren't expecting company."

"I don't care," she echoed the words back to him a second before she planted a hot, wet kiss on his mouth.

Opening her lips, she begged him to come inside. He obliged immediately, tasting every recess of her mouth as if she were his last meal. Or his first. Her hands were everywhere at once. One cupped his ass, pulling his erection closer to the soft mound between her thighs. Her other scraped beneath his shirt, trailing her nails over one painfully erect nipple. She pinched it and he winced.

He didn't want to feel anything but skin. He drew the straps of her tank-top down, almost trapping her upper arms against her body, then unhooked the thin strip of lace that made up her bra. Instantly, her breasts lunged into his hands. He broke their kiss and gently bit one of her aroused nipples, flicking his tongue over the peak, then softened the effect by laving a wide circle over the darkened flesh around it.

Every part of his body that had been neglected for the past ten years screamed for more. None moreso than his engorged cock. Blood rushed through him, which didn't seem possible since most of his blood supply had to be in his dick already.

Still, he wanted more. He wanted all of her.

Drawing the short skirt higher on her thigh, he groaned when he encountered the top of her thigh-high stocking. This was too unreal. Too perfect. His cock leapt and pulsed, begging to get out of his pants.

He spun her around and laid her on the worn sofa. Without invitation, her legs fell to the side. "You naughty girl," he said with a playful smirk. "You've done this before."

She laughed, batting her eyelashes while she drew her red-tipped fingernails gently over the soft flesh inside her thighs. "Who? Me?"

The material in her skirt rose higher to reveal a glistening pink slit between her legs. Smooth and wet, her clitoris beckoned to him.

When she sat up straight, effectively hiding her pussy, he experienced physical pain from the loss.

It didn't last long, however, as her nimble fingers made short work of the buttons on his jeans. His cock sprang free and it felt even better than walking out of the prison gate that morning. That was just his freedom.

This was pure liberation!

Her mouth fell around the head. Her tongue swirled masterfully until she squeezed more of his shaft into her mouth. Groaning, she struggled to fit more and more inside. Finally, she took him into her throat and gently worked her muscles around his cock.

He could die. He could die right this minute and he wouldn't give a flying fuck. His head fell back and he allowed himself to just feel.

It had been far too long since he'd buried his cock into a woman's willing, pliant body. Once, seven years ago, he'd fucked one of the lady-guards. But that was seven long-fucking-years.

Gently moving her head back and forth, she played with his dick like it was her favorite toy. She slid him out of her mouth, circled the head with the tip of her tongue before licking from the base to the tip in one long, steady draw. One hand cupped his ballsack, carefully scraping it with her nails. The other pumped his cock like a piston for a few strokes before she lowered her mouth over it again. Before long, she'd worked him into a state of near euphoria, his knees weakened from the expert attention she paid to him. He thrust into her mouth, over and over again. She encouraged him by gripping his ass in both hands and guiding his movements.

He could barely breathe. "God . . . you're good at . . . this."

Gradually, a familiar pressure built behind his cock. Any minute now, he was going to come, but he didn't want to. Not . . . yet. Too . . . soon.

He tore his dick from her mouth, stifling the self-imposed groan that followed. "Your turn."

"What?" Her voice was raw and, if he wasn't mistaken, more than a little surprised.

"What do you mean 'what'?" He chuckled, taking her hands and bringing her to her feet. Her body was full and womanly with curves in all the right places, from her thighs to her breasts. "Stand right here."

Her brown eyes bore into his with something akin to wonder. He finally broke the thick, heavy net she cast in his direction and licked his lips, already tasting the sweet come he'd seen promised between her legs. He sat on the sofa and slid his jeans further down his legs, finally shucking his books and kicking his jeans off.

With a modicum of gentle urging on his part, Lynn climbed over him and stood on the cushions until her pussy floated directly in front of his face. He inhaled the rich, musky scent of sex and woman before taking her ass in both hands and drawing her crotch against his mouth. He slid his tongue between the silken folds and nearly lost his breath when he found her clit. Swollen and ready, it practically burst in his mouth, like a sweet, plump grape.

Her hips moved in a steady rhythm, making love to his tongue while he delved and played within.

Sliding his tongue from her opening to her clit and back again, he devoured the sweet pleasure that was as much his as hers. A shudder fell over him. God, he couldn't come yet!

He grasped the base of his cock and squeezed, concentrating on bringing her to a dripping climax before he came. After a few minutes, her hands landed on his head and held his face against her. Thrusting against his tongue, she was a wild woman. Deliberately, he found her opening and pushed his tongue inside. She gasped and increased the speed of her hips.

When he glanced upward, her breasts swayed and her hair was a tangled mass that floated and curled around a face lost in the throes of near ecstasy. Delicately, he spread her ass cheeks. He delved two fingers inside her opening as he continued to lavish attention on her clitoris. She humped his fingers for a moment, until he removed them and traced a moist path to her anus. Fondling at first, he relished the sound of her increased moaning while he traced around the outside.

Taking advantage of his need for a deep, cleansing breath, he asked, "Yes?"

She seemed to know exactly what he meant, her eyes glowing with renewed anticipation. "Yes! God, yes. Do it!"

He clasped his lips on her pussy again at the same time he immersed the tip of one finger inside her anus.

Lynn threw her head back and screamed her release just as her pussy throbbed against his tongue. Her juices really did taste sweeter than wine.

Panting, Lynn fell to her knees, straddling the biker's thighs. Her tits were fuller, heavier, than she'd ever remembered them. Something tore at her insides. Desire? Lust? She didn't know, but it was more powerful than the worst of the New Sahara storms that brought mayhem and annihilation across the plains every summer. And it burned just as hot and just as destructive.

The feeling swam in her veins, overpowering her mind. Her blood boiled and her lungs seemed incapable of a full breath.

The desire ruled her. While she caught her breath, her hips moved closer to his massive cock. The slick, hot flesh between her legs touched his shaft. She almost lost it. Again. Right then, like a fucking geyser.

How had this happened to her? To her? A professional, damn it. The whimper that formed in her chest and whispered between her clenched teeth came as much from the erotic stirrings in her belly as it did from the unfamiliar doubt that chastised her with every silken thrust.

Camion froze. "What's wrong?"

She shook off the rising concern. She didn't want to feel anything expect his cock inside of her. "Nothing, cowboy."

"No, it's something."

She canted her head and bit her bottom lip as she raised herself slightly. "It's nothing, really."

He didn't believe her. She could see it in his eyes. "You're sure?"

Nodding, she arched her back. "Please, don't stop."

He took the tip of one breast into his mouth, laving her nipple before gently biting the peak and flicking his tongue over it. She groaned and tossed her head back while she impaled herself on his cock.

The frenzied sex was gone. She rode him slowly, savoring every moment. The biker raised his hips to meet her, barely containing his obvious need to take her faster; harder.   Lynn's hands rested on his shoulders and she arched her back even more, allowing herself to bring him farther inside. Soft mewling sounds came from her throat when she ground herself against him. Her flesh burned. Her mind reeled.

Gradually, she increased the pace. Instead of long, slow, incredibly deep thrusts, she rode him hard. Her fingernails bit into the tense muscles of his wide shoulders. She rocked her hips. Faster. Faster. And faster. When she looked into his eyes, he returned her gaze with a penetrating stare. It was as though he could read her soul, and he liked what he found.

No one had ever looked at her quite like that before.

A wave of pure ecstasy flowed over her, heating her skin from the inside out. Her womb clenched against itself. Her crotch wept with sheer delight. "Oh, God," she groaned. "Yes, yes, yes."

He grunted, thrusting hard against her G-spot every time the sway of her hips brought it within reach. "Come for me one more time, Lynn," he ordered. "Let yourself go, ahhh."

"I'm coming," she panted. "I'm coming again!" She arched her back one final time as wave after wave of an explosive climax made her tremble uncontrollably.

A moment later, after he'd milked every throbbing ounce of life from her very core, he released himself deep within her.

Perfect and pure. Blissful and oh-so-right.

Oh-so-terribly wrong.

Chapter Three

Lynn followed the biker through the back hallway behind the bar. Her entire body thrummed, from the ends of her hair to her fingertips, over her still-clenching womb, to the soles of her feet. It wasn't supposed to happen like this. She was supposed to remain in complete control. He was supposed to come for her, but not . . .

She tried to shake off the realization of all that had happened. It was too late now.

The man stopped suddenly and Lynn walked into his back. He spun to face her. His dark eyes sparkling their intent a second before he pressed her firmly against the wall, embracing her with his entire body while he took her mouth in a deeply erotic kiss. Slower, more deliberate than the other kisses they'd shared, he devoured her. His hands remained on the wall over her head while his body held hers solidly in place. Her hands, however, betrayed everything she'd ever known, all of her training and discipline, when they climbed over his sides and finally encircled his neck. She drew him closer, unable to withstand the growing need that, even now, suckled in her belly.

Breathless, he pulled away, piercing her to the wall with a simple gaze. "My name is Camion."

Her voice vanished. Her lips dried out. Her tongue swelled to four times its normal size. She meant the words to come out steady and strong. Confident. Instead, she croaked, "I don't care."

A knowing smile spread those soft, pliant lips so incredibly capable of bringing her to her knees. He shook his head and led her back into the main bar room.

"Damn. Who the hell are you ladies?" Camion stopped short in the doorway.

Lynn peered around him, then slipped past.

Three of the four bikers who'd been in the back of the room sat in the booth, their heads in their hands and their pants still around their knees. The fourth was lying in the middle of the pool table, obviously trying to catch his breath, completely naked.

The other bartender was nowhere to be seen.

Just then, the door opened and Reese, her commanding officer, and the other bartender stepped through. The bartender looked as if he'd been put through a wringer, his long black hair in shambles around shirtless shoulders. When his eyes fell on Camion, he straightened his posture and limped behind the bar. "Hey, bro."

"Hey," Camion replied with a curious glance at his friend. "Does any of this strike you as odd?"

"Odd? I don't know. But I'm more inclined to believe the letters-to-the-editor in Playboy from now on."

"Well, it's been fun, boys, but we better get going." Reese waved to Rebecca and Zimmer, two of their Project Specialists on this trip. "Let's get out of here."

Zimmer finished reapplying a dark burgundy lipstick before she smiled at Camion, waved to the men in the back, and sauntered out of the door, just in front of Lynn.

Outside, the world seemed a little brighter. Sure, the sun was huge and hot and baked the sleepy little town until it was crispy. But that didn't change the fact that Lynn had screwed up. She never screwed up! In almost six years as an officer in the United States Navy, she'd never once screwed up an assignment! *Damn* it.

Reese climbed into the motorhome they'd obtained from their contact in Salt Lake City. They would drive back to their landing zone in the Salt Flats, just outside of Tooele, Utah, tonight, then tomorrow they would begin their experiments. If the collections proved promising, they'd return to the bar this weekend, track their subjects, and finish the job.

"Be sure to put your specimens in the cooler, ladies. It's a long drive home." Reese placed her vial in the tiny refrigerator. Rebecca and Zimmer followed.

Lynn sat at the dinette table and dropped her forehead into her hands. "Fuck."

"Lynn, what's wrong? Where's your sample."

"You don't want to know," she mumbled, half-hoping only the table's laminate surface would hear.

"Oh, God, Lynn," whined Zimmer. "You didn't!"

"Uh-huh."

Lynn didn't have to look up to know that Reese had folded her arms over her barely concealed breasts and towered to her full five-foot-nine height. She could feel it in the shift of the stagnant air. "How did you let that happen?"

"Camion was so amazing," she whispered into her hands.

"Camion? You let him tell you his name? And what happens if he is a good one? What then? God, I can't believe you forgot something so fucking basic, Lynn. You have to stay distant. What happens if he's acceptable? How in hell are you going to separate this little friendship you have going from turning him over when we get back?"

"I can still do my job." She snapped her eyes in Reese's direction. "So I fucked up. I can fix this."

"How?" Reese all but tapped her pointed little shoes on the plastic runner covering the carpet.

Lynn scanned the motorhome. Zimmer eyed her with the smallest amount of sympathy in her gray eyes. Rebecca stared at her fingertips, apparently finding something very interesting in the pattern of her fingerprints. Lynn sighed. "Leave me behind. I can fix this. There's a hotel at the edge of town. I'll stay there, find him and get my sample." She stood, prepared to leave the motorhome and hike to the nearest dive motel. "Odds are good that at least one of the others is a match and you can pick me up this weekend."

Reese waved one perfectly manicured hand. "Forget it. What's done is done. We don't need him."

Something screamed denial inside of Lynn. *She* needed him.

No!

She needed to make this right. To prove to the others she'd kept her distance after all. To prove to herself that she hadn't lost her touch. It had nothing to do with how she'd come apart in Camion's arms, or the way he made her feel as though she were the most beautiful woman in four galaxies.

A shudder of remembered passion rocked her center off its axis.

It would be so much easier if they could simply harvest the men's seed and artificially inseminate women when they got back to their own time. But Artificial Insemination was illegal in the next millennium. It was that practice which had brought the near extinction of their race to begin with.

Lynn held her breath, but stood her ground. "I can fix this." She had to. She had to prove she could still hunt. If she went home without that single, tangible fact firmly in place, she'd be kicked out of the Navy sooner than she could blink.

And if she lost her job, she was as good as dead. Literally.

Sterile women were of absolutely no use to anyone, and therefore, were immediately put to death.

Chapter Four

Lynn curled into a ball in the back of the speeding motorhome. She pulled the blanket over her head and tried desperately not to cry. Or scream. Or beg for her life. It was her fault. She was the one who'd lost her edge and failed in her mission. A mission far too important to take lightly. The future of their race was at stake, for crying out loud.

Manhunters had been in place for only four months. The census bureau had been the first to notice a decline in male births, fifty years ago, and when they'd compared their numbers with the statistics from other countries around the globe, the catastrophic conclusion had been painfully simple. Years of genetic altering and artificial inseminations – put together with the practice of 'designer' children – and the human animal had been drastically altered. Even with increased manipulation, there hadn't been a healthy male child born anywhere in the world in twenty-five years. Her own brother had been the last. Since then, there had been the occasional boy-child, but so grossly malformed that they hadn't survived infancy.

If something didn't happen soon to change things, the human species would drown in its own genetic cesspool.

The President of the United States, ironically a man and the father of twelve daughters himself, had commissioned the Manhunters as a Special Forces division of the United States Navy, like the SEALs of old. Their job was to travel through the recently harnessed wormhole just outside the Earth's atmosphere and collect breeding stock.

Men.

Men with unaltered genes.

They couldn't simply collect the semen, however. They had to have the whole man, otherwise, the genetic splicing that wreaked such havoc on the world might continue. At present, there were three colonies set up to house the breeders. Amazonia, Sarmatia, and Sirenus. Sarmatia and Sirenus remained empty, waiting the first of their citizens. Amazonia already had several men, all of whom were predisposed to bearing male children. Since the first mission, two months ago, more than seventy-five female breeders had been impregnated. Early tests promised that sixty-three of them were boys.

It was the Manhunters' job to fill the colonies with breeding stock to ensure the survival of the race. It wasn't her job to fall for a pasttimer, like a school girl with a fucking crush!

Lynn had been an outstanding Naval officer for six, long years. She'd been hand selected to serve in the Manhunters because of her love of American history and her ability to blend into the oldtimes. This was her third mission.

She should have been able to do her job. Gather the evidence. Analyze it. Act.

So why did she feel as though someone had ripped her heart out with a rusted spoon?

* * *

Camion hung back as far as he could and still keep the motorhome in sight. So long as they didn't leave Utah, he would be fine. But what if they crossed the state line? Would he jeopardize his parole to follow her? A woman he'd barely met?

He studied the road and weaved his bike around a slow-moving Jetta in front of him. Yep. He'd follow her to the fucking moon.

Something wasn't quite right. Women – particularly beautiful women – didn't show up in bars in the middle of a Tuesday, dressed like sin on a stick, and seduce a room full of strangers.

As soon as they'd left, he'd clapped his brother on the back and expressed his gratitude with a silent, knowing smile. "Way to go, man."

"What?" Con answered, incredulous. "What are you thanking me for?"

"You hired them, right? A welcome home gift?"

Con shook his head. "No way."

"C'mon, bro. How much did it set you back?"

"They weren't hookers, man. I'm tellin' ya. Did you pay them anything?"

"No."

"Neither did I. Hey, you," Con called to the man just climbing off the pool table. "You pay those chicks?"

The stranger shook his head, more inebriated from the treatment he'd just received than any of the booze he'd been downing most of the morning.

"Something doesn't add up here." Camion crossed to the window at the end of the bar and moved the heavy drapery aside. The motorhome was still in the parking lot. Nobody sat at the wheel yet. He could just make out the tall redhead who'd shown his brother such a good time standing with her back to the huge, globe-like front windows.

"You know what's weird? She wouldn't let me fuck her. I mean, she did all sorts of . . . well, you know. But it had to be her way. And her way was doing all the deeds herself."

"Sure, but who gives a shit," snorted one of the customers. He slid up to the bar and tapped on the surface. Con set a chilled bottle of beer in front of him before the biker continued. "I didn't even care about the blindfold."

"Blindfold?" Camion was more intrigued by the minute.

"Sorry, was that just our girls? They blindfolded all three of us."

"Me, too," added Con.

Camion looked out the window again. Red threw

herself behind the wheel, obviously hotter than Hades about something. Behind her, Lynn ran to the back of the camper and slammed the partition to the bedroom.

"I wasn't blindfolded. And I fucked the shit out of her."

That was when he'd made the decision something was very wrong. He'd climbed on his bike and for the last seven hours, he'd followed the strange women all the way to the Salt Flats.

Finally, the motorhome turned off I-80 and headed into the huge expanse of nothing that made up the flats.

With no moon, the night loomed black as coal. He gave them a headstart, then followed the glowing red taillights into oblivion.

There were no campgrounds – no camp*sites* – on the Flats. Nothing of interest, at all. What would four sexkittens do this far from nowhere? Twenty miles later, the motorhome stopped, its brakes squealing in protest at the amount of salt that had more than likely settled on the drums.

Camion squinted into the distance and drew his bike to a halt several hundred feet shy of the camper. The stars twinkled overhead, but for the second time in thirty minutes, he was thankful for no moon.

Except he couldn't see shit.

Leaving his bike behind, he crept closer to where the women were parked. Stilted voices hovered on the still night air like voices of ghosts. He approached the motorhome from their blindside. Slowly. When he reached it, he peeked in a side window.

Nobody home.

He circled the vehicle and peered around the front end.

His jaw dropped.

What the hell . . .?

Sitting on the desert floor like a giant . . . he

didn't know what . . . was a plane. Kind of. Silver with what looked like an anchor painted on the nose, the craft looked like a cross between a plane and rocket, with huge jet engines in the rear. The engines, or exhausts maybe, were stained black and had more than a few dents. The plane's body was also dented, dirty, and looked like it had seen better days.

There were no tires. No wheels.

It had apparently touched down vertically to rest on four legs. That was all he could call them. Legs.

Every badly-produced Science Fiction based porn movie he'd watched came rushing back. *Bimbos From Planet X Do Utah #76?* Yeah, right. She hadn't fucked like an alien, so there had to be some other explanation.

In any case, something was *very* wrong.

"Freeze."

Camion didn't turn around. Instead, he stood tall, lifting his hands from his sides. "You've got to be kidding," he sighed.

"Don't move a muscle, buddy. I'll paint the desert with your ass."

He shook his head. He must have stumbled on some top-secret experiment from Area 51 or Dugway.

This was just what he needed.

"How did you get here?"

"Ask whoever was driving that rig. I've been tailing you since Pleasant. You know, if you're trying to maintain a low profile, you might have picked a different vehicle."

"Kenya, what's going on?" Red called from inside the . . . ship.

"Intruder, ma'am!"

Several pairs of footsteps clamored down a ramp extending from the belly of the plane. Lynn and her companions stood wide-eyed in front of him.

Red grimaced. "Fuck!"

One of the girls from the bar held up her hands

in a defensive posture. "This isn't a problem. We just hold him until we get the others and--"

"Are you out of your mind, Zimmer? Hold him? We're officers in the United States Navy, not kidnappers."

The woman called Zimmer rolled her eyes. "Actually, we're basically pirates."

"Privateers," called the woman behind him.

"Whatever the hell you are, I'm not bounty, so let's call it a night, shall we?" Camion took a step backward, toward the voice.

"So what do we do?" asked the one called Zimmer.

Red shrugged. "Abort."

"Reese. Come on. We can't abort. We need to analyze the specimens and make the harvest as needed," Lynn declared.

Another step.

"So you suggest we do what?" Reese threw her hands in the air.

"We finish our mission!"

Another step.

Utilizing all of the training he'd been given in his youth, Camion spun in a sweeping circle, kicking out one leg. He caught the fifth woman's shin, knocking her to the ground. Effective, concise movements followed. He grabbed the odd looking gun she'd dropped as she fell, pressed it at point-blank range to her throat, and held her down with one knee on her chest. "We're going to stand up. Slowly."

She nodded.

Hushed stillness swallowed the desert.

Once on his feet, he helped his hostage to hers.

Cripes. His hostage. How was it he ended up in situations like this? What was it about his sign, or his destiny, or his fucking-bad luck that made him a target for some cosmic joke?

"Don't do anything you'll be sorry for." Reese's voice sounded like she spoke to a child. "Put the gun down. Let Kenya go and we can just go our separate ways."

"Right. Like that's gonna happen, lady. I don't know who you are, but I cut my teeth on this next-level shit when you were still in grammar school. No way can you turn your back on me now."

"You won't say anything, right? 'Cause nobody will believe you."

"Not playing that game. I've got too much to lose. So here's the deal. Lynn over there and I are going for a little walk. When I feel like I'm safe, I'll drop her somewhere and you can pick her up."

Reese frowned while she seemed to consider his words. Finally, she responded – cold and lifeless. "Fine. Take her. Kenya, get your ass over here."

Lynn gasped. "Excuse me?"

"Go, Lieutenant. This is all your fault anyway."

Lieutenant, huh? Well, at least he outranked her. Or, he used to.

Grumbling something under her breath, Lynn

traded places with Kenya. He grabbed her arm and dragged her against his chest. Immediate stirrings surged through his cock. No matter what was going on, one thing was crystal clear. He wanted her again.

Without taking his eyes off the women, he backed away. Together, he and Lynn walked backwards until enough distance separated them from the others. Then he turned, grabbed Lynn by the hand, and ran to his bike. Lynn managed to keep pace with him, but then, he'd shortened his strides to accommodate for her smaller size. Once they reached his motorcycle, he climbed on and handed her his helmet. "Get on."

"You can leave me here. I promise we won't--"

He silenced her with a glare. Reluctantly, she climbed on the bike behind him, the helmet dwarfing her head. "Hang on tight, whoever-the-hell-you-are. It's gonna be a bumpy ride."

Lynn held onto Camion for all she was worth. He hadn't been lying. The Salt Flats might be flat, but they were anything but smooth. By the time they hit the main road, she wasn't sure she had any teeth left.

Camion turned onto the highway and headed farther away from Salt Lake. Lynn held him tightly around his lower chest, her arms unable to complete the circle. Even through the leather jacket he wore, the thick muscles of his back were plainly evident when he shifted through the gears and brought the bike to a roaring, deafening speed. Waves of desire pulsed through her, enhanced by the vibrating machine between her legs. Her breasts, pressed against his rippling back, peaked with anticipation.

She fought the heat that wound through her veins. She had more important things to thing about. Like where he was taking her. "We should go back to Pleasant!" she screamed over the wind, her voice raw and dry.

"Not likely!"

A few miles up the highway, he slowed and turned onto a one-lane dirt road. A few more jarring miles, and he guided his bike into a narrow canyon. Huge, dark rockfaces enclosed them in a tomb of echoing stillness. Scrub brush lined the trail – it had ceased being a road more than a mile before – while oddly shaped trees grew from the rock walls. Somewhere in the distance, an animal cried its displeasure at the human intrusion.

Finally, Camion stopped and climbed off the bike. "Get off."

"You know, you don't have to be quite so rude."

"Oh, I don't? Hmm, let me think." He tilted his enchanting blue eyes upward for a moment, before stabbing her with an annoyed glare. "Tough."

"What's wrong with you?"

"I don't like being played for a fool. What kind of sick game are you and your galpals playing?"

"It's classified."

"Yeah. Right. I'll just bet it is. *Lieutenant.*" He

pointed to an impossibly small crevice in the rock strata. "March."

Not one for patience, he shoved her shoulder.

Lynn sucked in a breath. If he'd wanted her dead, he would have killed her already. And it's not as if Reese didn't know where they were. If she knew her commanding officer like she thought she did, Reese was already tracking their location with the beacon she'd planted on Camion back at the bar. That was, if he hadn't found it and removed it already.

Damn. This wasn't going well, at all.

Struggling against the rough canyon walls, she forced herself through the crevice. Only a couple of feet deep, it opened in a valley. Starlight sparkled off a large spring and reflected on the walls of a tiny cabin. It was as though she'd walked back in time. Again. No longer in the twenty-first century, she'd stepped into the nineteenth. The old miner's cabin appeared no larger than the main living quarters on

The Holy Grail. The roof lifted on one side, the shingles torn and ugly. The porch sagged. The sole window was broken in two places.

But it was beautiful. She stole a breath. "Where is this place?"

"I call it the 'Hole in the Wall', but it's not really. That's much farther south. But it's as good a hideout as any."

"Hole in the wall? You mean the hideout for Butch Cassidy and the Sun Dancer?"

Camion laughed, shaking his head and bringing a lock of hair over his left eye. "The Sundance Kid. Not the Sun Dancer. Where the hell are you from anyway?"

He led her inside the dingy, dusty interior of the cabin. A bed against the far wall took up most of the room. Between that, and the rickety table beneath the window, there was barely enough room to stand. Suddenly, Camion seemed even larger than his six-foot-three-inches.

"Are you hungry?"

She snapped her attention away from the not-so-subtle stirrings in her belly. "What?"

"Food. Do you want some food?"

Camion opened a cupboard that hung over a rusted cook stove. From inside the dusty shelves, he withdrew a large, filthy can. She made a face and turned away. "I'll pass."

"Suit yourself."

The sound of a manual can-opener filled the small room. At least it pushed away the unease that being along with him again brought. Without a word, he slid past her and left the cabin.

Should she follow?

She half-snorted. She should be looking for a way out, but something told her his lightening reflexes would capture her before she could reach the tiny pathway that was her only escape. Instead, she sat on the bed and rested her elbows on her knees. With her head in her hands, she studied the uneven floor, littered with dust bunnies and scraps of paper.

One piece of paper caught her attention. "Fit Rep Camion Drake," she muttered, reading the words through the smudged boot prints. She picked it up, her fingers trembling. "Department of the Navy. July Eighteenth, Nineteen Ninety Six. Commander Drake has exhibited behavior unsuitable for an officer and a gentleman. He has been found guilty of violating Articles 118, 120 and 89 of the Uniform Code of Military Justice. His continued forceful objections are duly noted, however it is the recommendation of this governing body that Commander Drake be removed from command and sentenced to life imprisonment with hard labor without the possibility of . . . "

"What are you reading?"

CHAPTER FIVE

Camion's voice bit into the back of her head and she winced. "Nothing," she half-shouted, tossing the report on the floor while she spun to face him.

He held two bowls in strong, capable hands. No tremors affected him. He didn't look even a little nervous, despite the fact he'd kidnapped her. Calm. Collected. Perfect. That was Commander Camion Drake.

Raising an eyebrow while he indicated the outside of the cabin with a slight nod, he pinned her with a solid, knowing glare. "I thought you might change your mind about dinner. It's nicer outside. C'mon."

"What are you going to do with me?"

His glare turned into something warmer, gentler, and infinitely more threatening. "That's a loaded question if I ever heard one."

She swallowed at the implication of his words. "You can't keep me here."

"Sure I can. Let's eat."

He left the cabin again. Lynn quickly collected the report, folded it, and tucked it into her skirt pocket before she followed him outside.

"The others will come after me, you know."

"I'm sure they will." Camion settled on the fallen trunk of a tree and ate his canned dinner as though he were a starving refugee.

"You know I'm an officer in the United States Navy. You're committing a federal offense by holding me against my will."

With the bowl of his plastic spoon, he pointed toward the crevice through which they'd traveled to reach the spring. "Feel free to hike back."

"Don't be ridiculous. It's dark and I don't know the area. We're kilometers from civilization."

He shrugged, pulling the fabric of his shirt tight

over the rounded muscles on his upper arms and shoulders. "Suit yourself."

"Don't be obtuse. You know I'm not going to leave."

"If you're not going to leave, I suggest you eat something."

He put his empty bowl aside and stood. "I'm going to take a dip. Watch out for snakes and scorpions."

Casually, as though he didn't have a single concern in the world, he strolled to the edge of the spring and stripped. Shirt, boots. Jeans. All gone.

Naked, he was glorious; even from the back. The tight muscles of his ass bunched when he walked proudly along the bank and climbed onto a large, red boulder that looked black in the night air. The dry, desert wind lifted his hair just as he glanced at the rising moon. Then he leapt. For a moment, she thought he might actually be capable of flight, his golden body practically glistening in the soft, white light. He dove beautifully into the still waters, disappearing beneath the surface with barely a splash.

She could leave. He'd said so. Her survival training would bring her safely back to her crew. It really didn't matter that is was dark. From there, she could face the consequences of her actions.

She could leave.

But she didn't want to.

* * *

Camion studied Lynn over the top of a cup of bitter, stale coffee. Night had fallen more than an hour earlier and their shared campfire blazed bright orange. It cast glowing light on Lynn's face, even as the shifting shadows of the trees danced on the tall, canyon walls.

So far, she'd played it pretty cool. She hadn't tried to leave, even when he'd told her she could.

He lowered the cup and rested his forearm on his raised knee, half-reclining on his other elbow. Part of him wished she would try to run so he could catch her and feel her full curves against him again. The taste she'd given him earlier in the day wasn't nearly enough to satisfy the endless craving that made his cock harder than the rocks circling the fire. That's why he'd gone for a swim – hoping the chilling, frigid water would put a damper on the fact he wanted her more than he'd ever wanted anything in his life. It hadn't worked.

Man, she's beautiful.

The thought invaded with the force of a sledgehammer. He frowned while tiny winged creatures took up residence in his gut. What was it about her that captivated him? The way her eyes never stopped searching for . . . something? The gentle slope of her breasts, or the sparks of light that danced in her irises when she looked at him? Hell, he didn't know.

"How long were you in the Navy?"

He snapped his gaze to her face, the urge to tell her to mind her own business mixing with the urge to kiss her senseless by way of changing the damned subject.

"Too long," he replied, instead.

Of all the scraps of his former life inside the cabin, she had to find his last Fitness Report. More bad karma, he supposed.

"You were in prison. You mentioned that . . . before. Ten years, was it?"

"I don't like to talk about it."

"So you were in the Navy, and ended up in prison."

He sighed and rubbed his hand over his jaw, scratching the stubble that itched almost as much as her stare. She wasn't going to let him off the hook, was she? "I was a SEAL."

"Sea, Air, and Land . . . Hooah."

"Very good. Not many people know what it

stands for."

"They offered me a slot when I was in Candidate School, but I thought . . . nah."

He raised an eyebrow. "You're a woman."

Lynn bit her lip for a split second and appeared almost frightened. She covered immediately, however, rolling her eyes. "I was kidding." Sobering, she added, "Tell me about your last mission."

"No thanks."

"Come on. What else is there to talk about?"

He could think of a million other things. And a million more that involved no talking at all.

"I found the Fit-Rep. You came here when they started hunting you, didn't you? You were sentenced to life in prison, yet, here you are."

He sighed, picking up a stick and throwing it on the fire. Her eyes bore through him, telling him she wasn't going to give up anytime soon. He picked up another stick, broke it and placed it outside the fire pit. "We were in a part of the world we weren't supposed to be in. The War on Drugs was over, for all intents and purposes, but only on the surface. We still went into Central America on the sly and took out as many drug operations as we could without having to explain the budget to Congress."

"I read about operations like that. No backup. Firefights."

"Yeah, well, one particular op raised my awareness more than others. My C.O. was a real asshole. I never liked him, but even I didn't realize what he was up to."

"What was he up to?"

"Slave trafficking."

"You're kidding!"

"I wish. Nope. He was working with some lowlifes in the cities to kidnap young women and transport them to the drug factories in the bush. They were house entertainment for the guards and rewards for the workers."

"That's terrible," she breathed. "What was your boss getting out of it?"

"Money, of course. He knew where the camps were and whenever we were sent in-country to take out the bad guys, he'd lead us away from his friends. He was paid a pretty penny, and he got the girls when they were finished with them."

"And you found out about him."

"Bingo. We were bivouacked for the night. Raining like a sonofabitch. Muggy as hell. I was on watch and saw Fletcher sneak out of camp. I shouldn't have, but I followed him. About a half-click outside of our perimeter, he met three locals. Beefy guys. Ugly as sin. They acted like they'd been buddies for years. I remember feeling my MRE back up on me. It was disgusting."

"Did you confront him?"

"No. I was outmanned and outgunned. I planned to report him when we got back to the world, but then . . ."

"Go on," Lynn urged.

Something in her eyes made him trust her. Made him think she might actually believe him, since no one else had at the time. That mysterious something made him continue even if he didn't understand why.

"They pushed a girl at him. I hadn't seen her at first because she was hidden behind the locals. She was young, maybe twenty, or so. Long, black hair all matted and tangled and she had a bruise on her cheek. A cut on her lip was still bleeding. The guys left and Fletcher had the girl on the ground in a matter of seconds."

"He didn't rape her!"

"I got there as fast as I could. I didn't care about what it would mean to my future. Hell, he was assaulting her right in front of me. What was I supposed to do?"

"You stopped him."

A bitter laugh swelled in Camion's chest. "I

stopped him, all right. I pulled my weapon, shoved the barrel into his face and ordered him to his feet. He laughed. The sonofabitch laughed at me.

"His friend's hadn't really left. They jumped me from behind. I thought I was dead. I really did. Instead, Fletcher and the locals argued in Spanish for a few minutes. Fletcher pointed his sidearm at my head, then moved it away just before he shot one of his buddies right between the eyes. He took all three of them out in three seconds flat, then shot the girl. Then he pistol-whipped me."

"Camion." Lynn's voice was full of compassion and tightly-controlled fury. It made the last ten years worth it. Almost.

"I'm sure you can figure out the rest."

"He claimed he found you with the girl, and the drug dealers, didn't he?"

"Bingo, again. They found traces of gunpowder residue on my hands. They found female DNA on my clothes, but of course they didn't have her body to examine or they would have found Fletcher's DNA all over her. It was his word against mine. He claimed he followed me leaving my post."

"And you went to prison. Did you escape? Is that what's happening here?"

Camion smiled. She wasn't judging him. Only curiosity colored her words. "No. I didn't escape. Fletcher got busted about a year ago for whatever his latest scheme was. Two months ago, he shot himself in his quarters and left behind all of his journals, including the one detailing how he framed me. The sonofabitch was writing a goddamned screenplay about it." He shook his head, still unwilling to believe it himself. "Anyway, it took a few weeks to process me out, and yesterday morning I walked out of Leavenworth almost a free man."

"Almost?"

"Oh yeah, the government doesn't like to admit its wrong no matter what. So I'm on parole, technically. I was still guilty of disrespecting a superior officer."

"You can't possibly mean Fletcher?" she rebutted in disbelief.

"No, not Fletcher. When they sentenced me, I stormed the bench and knocked the judge out cold." Somewhere along the line, she'd moved next to him. He could feel her heat wrap him like loving arms. "Why aren't you terrified? Why aren't you running for your life right about now?"

She glanced at him and his heart pounded. "You're not going to hurt me, Drake. Any fool could see that. Though, I'll admit, I'm a little curious about what you plan to do next."

"It's late. I think we should go to bed." He stretched next to her, brushing a wisp of hair out of her eyes. Such amazing eyes, he thought.

Lynn couldn't take her eyes off Camion. He stared at her as if he'd never seen a woman before. As if she were some kind of angel. She liked it, and despite herself, she liked him. A lot.

Tomorrow would bring Reese and the others to their quiet, secluded world, but Lynn wanted this one night to fully explore the powerful urges that raced through her sensual side. Not just sexual. This wasn't about breeding. It was stronger and more powerful.

He pulled a course rope from his jacket pocket. "Now, we both know you've been trained in situations like this. The minute I fall asleep, you'll try to find your way back to your shuttle, or whatever the hell it is. So, I'm doing this for your own good."

"Doing what?" She eyed the rope, then returned her attention to his face.

"You may think you want to wander around in the middle of the night, but you only think you do."

"I won't try to run, Camion. You don't have to do this."

He quirked an eyebrow. "I'll make the decisions

for the next little while. If I fall asleep, you'll disappear within seconds, and quite frankly, I'm tired as hell and don't want to stare at the fire, or you, for the next six hours. Give me your hands."

"No."

He took them anyway. She could have fought him. Probably should have, but the second his fingers wrapped around her wrists, electric pulses of light flew up her arm to settle in her breasts. Her nipples tightened. There was something freshly erotic about the thought of lying bound next to him for the rest of the night.

His movements were gentle and kind. When the rough cords scratched the soft flesh on the inside of her left wrist, he winced. But a few minutes later, Lynn found herself with both wrists tied together.

Conscious panic lodged in her throat. What the hell was wrong with her?

"Shh," he breathed. "I'm not going to hurt you." He cleared his throat. "In fact, I was going to tie you my waist, but . . ."

"But what?" If her heart beat any faster, it would explode.

A devious gleam entered his eyes, and his expression turned positively mischievous. "I have a better idea."

He lifted her as though she weighed nothing, collecting the blanket upon which she'd been sitting in the process. His arms, like bands of steel, bore her not-insignificant weight to the edge of the spring where he laid her on the soft sand. Then he spread the blanket along the bank. She moved to sit on it, and he grinned. "Anxious?"

She could only stare at him, standing over her like a god in some fantasy. A slight breeze lifted his hair off his shoulders. His eyes were intense and full of promise.

Promises of what? They couldn't make promises. She was being more than ridiculous to even consider such a thing. They had only this one night.

Camion tied the other end of the rope to the trunk of a tree several feet behind her. When he returned, he had lost his jacket and shirt, and his boots and his jeans were unbuttoned to reveal dark curls. Her gaze traveled over the smooth ridges of his chest and abdomen. Her temperature rose several notches just from the looking.

"Lie down," he half-whispered, half-ordered.

She obeyed. She didn't know why. Ever since she could remember, she'd been in charge. Maybe not the highest-ranking officer, but certainly in command of others. She could take orders, but normally, she didn't like it so much. The freedom that came with surrender was unlike any she'd ever known.

Once she settled onto the blanket, Camion dragged it farther from the base of the tree. Before she knew what was happening, her arms were stretched above her head. The ropes were just tight enough that she couldn't get up, but not so tight as to harm her wrists.

She fastened her gaze on Camion's face. He drew his attention over her with a hunger and appreciation that stole her breath. Then he grinned. "You're overdressed."

He knelt beside her on the blanket. Huge and overpowering, his size alone sent quivers through her. Slowly, he drew her shirt high – over her belly to reveal her bra and eventually along her arms until it caught in the knots at her wrist. As though she were the most delicate thing on the planet, he stripped her. A few moments later, she lay vulnerable and naked. Heat pooled between her legs. It was sweet, deliberate torture.

Camion's hands trembled. The hot, needy looks she sent him cut him clear to his DNA structure, rearranging everything he'd thought he'd known about himself. The distant fire crackled and sent rivers of yellow and orange light to illuminate the curve of one breast, one hip. Her legs writhed, begging for his touch.

Bad manners to keep a lady waiting, he thought.

Still kneeling at her dainty feet, the polished toes like tiny bits of candy, he ran his hands over the smooth surface of her calves. He purposefully memorized every inch, then parted them when he reached her knees. The pink flesh between her legs already glistened. "What do you want?" he asked.

She moaned. "Don't tease. I want your mouth on me. Now."

Shaking his head, he laughed. "I'm in charge, remember? I'm asking for suggestions, not orders." He stretched over her length, gasping silently when his chest met the tight buds of her hardened nipples. "Nevermind. I don't need any suggestions."

Like a hungry lion, he devoured her mouth. Lynn opened willingly, suckling his bottom lip and tracing her tongue over his. Below him, her supine body arched as though she tried to crawl inside of him. He tore his mouth away from her lips, sliding his hands up her arms before paying homage to her neck, her chest, and then the tip of one breast. He gently flicked his tongue over her nipple.

Lynn felt like she was having an out of body experience. This was her, lying beneath Camion, her body taut and willing, but it wasn't her. She didn't get emotionally involved with her subjects. Still, she couldn't deny that if – no, when – she gave him up she would never be the same.

He continued his trek over her body. He laved her nipples, sucking and biting and soothing, before moving lower to pay sweet, seductive homage to the soft area above her diaphragm. She wanted to wrap herself around him, but could only manage to bring her knees upward. Her hands were firmly out of her control, like everything else about this situation. So she brought her legs around his waist and thrust her hips. Her pussy scraped against the partially opened fly in his jeans, the thick denim teasing her core.

"More," she panted. "I want more."

"Demanding, aren't you?" His voice bore a confidence that made her insides even hotter. "All right. More it is."

Camion couldn't imagine anything closer to heaven than this woman writhing beneath him. Undeterred by Lynn's vice-like grip around his waist, he pushed her legs apart and completed his downward slide. When his mouth found her clitoris, the tiny bud pulsed against his tongue. She gasped, her hips dancing beneath his mouth so that he had to hold her hips firmly. Using his thumbs, he spread her pussy lips, exposing the soft, wet core to the night air. Her flesh glistened in the moonlight as tiny drops of dew collected around her vagina. When he returned his mouth to her, he licked long and slow from the opening to her clitoris and back, again and again. Before long, she strained against him, panting and moaning like a wild thing.

Her breasts thrust heavenward when she arched

her back. "I'm gonna come," she whispered through gritted teeth. "Oh, God, yes. I'm coming!"

The sound of her cries echoed off the canyon walls, reverberating through time and space. Before she finished, before her cries dissipated into the atmosphere, he was naked. He pulled his k-bar military knife from its sheath beside the blanket and sliced the ropes around her wrists. He wanted to feel her hands on him, wanted to .ffind his own ultimate freedom inside of her.

He entered with one hard and fast thrust. She pulsed around his cock, her legs capturing his waist at the same time her arms fell around his neck and shoulders. He froze. "Don't move," he whispered.

"I couldn't move if I tried," she replied, her voice as spent as the rest of her, apparently.

He chuckled, waiting for the initial unearthly sensations of her pussy wrapped around his cock to lessen so he could savor the event for the treasure it was. Pure, blissful rapture.

When his heart rate seemed under control and his muscles relaxed, he ground his hips against her. Heat, liquid and life-giving, floated through his veins. She undid him with only her presence, so when she thrust against him, he groaned. "You're trying to kill me, aren't you?"

"Never." But her satisfied grin told him she enjoyed the way he responded to her.

Gradually, the crescendo built in his gut. He moved faster, as though he kept pace with something outside of himself, something ancient.

Faster.

Harder.

Deeper.

Lost to the force that drove him, he gave everything to Lynn. His soul cried out to join with hers forever.

She arched against him, coming again. Her juices quenched a thirst he hadn't known was there until he met her. When the powerful urge to come slicked over his damp, night-chilled limbs, he didn't fight it. He poured himself into her. Throbbing and suddenly filled with light and hope, he allowed his soul the freedom to sing out her name.

How could he even think about letting her go?

Something icy fell over him. Someone was behind him. Lynn cursed.

Every muscle in his body tensed. Every highly-trained instinct told him to protect Lynn. He lunged to his knees, reaching for his knife.

Lynn scooted backward, struggling to her feet. "Reese! No!"

CHAPTER SIX

Groggy. Sleepy.

Camion shook off the feelings and honed his attention to his surroundings. His stomach lurched for a moment before settling again. Was he ill?

His back pressed against the thin mattress of his rack. The steel beneath bit into him with a vengeance he'd come to realize as his destiny, beginning with the day he'd decided to become a SEAL. What an ever-loving fool he'd been.

A vision swam behind his closed eyelids. Lynn. Strong, powerful, beautiful Lynn. But she couldn't be real. Not if . . .

It had all been a dream. He was still in prison.

Fuck.

No matter what nefarious shit his dream woman was into, he still wanted her. Just his luck she didn't even exist.

His cock hardened anyway. The good thing about being a government prisoner with secrets worth telling was the private accommodations. He might not be able to fuck her for real, but he could sure as hell dream about it. He tried to move his right hand to grab the base of his engorged dick.

His hand didn't move. Frowning, he pulled against whatever held him back.

Any sense of grogginess vanished. He opened his eyes, while he struggled against thick, braided cords that held his wrists and ankles firmly to the corners of a narrow rack. He quickly scanned the room. Gray. Battleship gray, actually. The room was small, with not one item to identify its regular occupant. No photographs taped the ceiling above the bed. No furniture other than the built in rack and a built in desk, if he could even call it that. A tiny, stainless steel sink had been embedded into a wall. Opposite the rack upon which he'd been not-so delicately tied, a full-length mirror hung on the only door. His reflection only pissed him off more. Not only was he tied to the bed. He was tied to the bed stark-ass naked.

He gritted his teeth and stared at the bare ceiling. As prison cells went, it was damned near luxurious, but if what he suspected was true, the Navy had come a long way in neglecting its officers.

A speaker by his head squawked. "If we come in, will you behave yourself?"

"Fuck you, bitch!"

Reese's voice answered. "You already did that, Mr. Drake. That's what got us into this mess in the first place."

The door opened. Reese filled the doorway, her shoulders back. Prime officer bearing. Totally in charge.

He knew the type and he didn't like it anymore now than he had a decade ago when his own commanding officer had fed him to the wolves.

Surprisingly, Reese stepped aside, permitting Lynn to come into the room. Before Reese closed the door, she said, "Lt. Ramsey . . . let's hope for the best. Do it right this time."

The door clicked shut behind Reese, leaving him alone with Lynn.

Lynn set a small pouch on the desk and crossed her arms. Covering her from head toe, the formfitting jumpsuit she wore accentuated each of her womanly curves. Her hair was loose, still a little damp as though she'd recently washed it. The soft scent of soap confirmed she'd taken a shower. The iridescent grayish-silver of her uniform highlighted her dark lashes and eyebrows, giving her a dominant quality that stirred his loins to an even fuller erection.

Fuck. They would have to decide who was going to be the boss if this relationship was going to work out.

"Do you know where you are?" Lynn's voice

was firm and steady. Almost . . . medicinal.

"I have a vague idea."

"You're aboard the USS Holy Grail, a Grail Class Time Ship. Our current heading is Earth and we should be there in no fewer than three hours. That turning you felt in your stomach a few minutes ago was this ship exiting the worm hole that connects our two time periods."

Camion shook his head to clear his hearing. He must have forgotten to take the bullshit out of his ears that morning. Time ship? Worm hole? "Excuse me?"

"Time travel, Mr. Drake. My colleagues and I work for the United States Government in the year three-thousand-twenty-seven."

"You're shittin' me, right?" He laughed. Okay, it all made sense now. It was a fucking joke. A reality show. Any minute now those two hot chicks from The Playboy Channel were going to poke their heads in and point out the cameras.

"I'm afraid not. Unfortunately," she paused and swallowed. Hard. "Because of you, I jeopardized our entire mission. So I'm here now to complete my job and with any luck, you will be equal parts my ruination and my savior."

"Complete your job?"

"Harvesting. I'm a Manhunter."

"Considering I'm a man, that doesn't sound very good."

She smiled. "You didn't seem to mind back in Pleasant, or at your cabin in the glen."

"Well, excuse the fuck out of me if things have changed a bit since the last time we fucked each other."

Okay, maybe that was a little harsh. Lynn's expression was strained and her eyes misted. "They're watching us, Camion," she whispered, her voice cracking on his name. "Please, just let me do my job. For both our sakes."

He scanned the ceiling again. The camera wasn't

hidden, after all. How had he missed it before? That tiny black dot on the ceiling above the bed.

Lynn's hands crawled over his chest, leaving tendrils of fire in their wake. Even now, he wanted her. Damn it to hell, he couldn't help himself. Something about her made his blood boil. While he should be figuring a way free of this mess, his cock had different ideas.

After a few teasing strokes over his abdomen, she cupped his balls with one hand and grasped his shaft with the other. He struggled against his bonds, unable to move his arms or his legs more than a few centimeters. His hips began to rock of their own accord, meeting the soft warmth of her palm while she plied her wicked magic. "Don't," he breathed.

"Come for me, Camion. You like my hands on you. Fuck my hands. Harder."

"No," he answered. He didn't know if he was arguing with her, or himself.

"Do it for me, Camion. Do it for us."

It was hopeless. Her hands on his body stole any pretense of rational thought. He became what she wanted; completely at her mercy. Faster and harder he met her ever-tightening grip. When a few drops of pre-come escaped the tip of his cock, she drew it onto his shaft, letting her hands glide smoothly over his heated flesh. Lifting her other hand away from his balls, she concentrated her efforts on giving him the best damned hand-job he'd ever had. His bones melted. His stomach clenched. "Don't stop!"

"I won't stop. I promise. Come, baby."

His mind reeled and exploded in millions of colors mixing in a brilliant dawn behind his closed eyes. But he forced his eyes open, anyway. He had to see her face, had to find the acknowledgment of what they shared in the blue of her eyes.

She stood over him, a glass vile in one hand. He squinted at the vile, filled with a white, creamy substance.

No way. "Is that . . ."

"The harvest. Just like I told you. It turns out that your brother would have made a terrific candidate for our breeding program. I can only hope, considering you're full brothers, that your analysis will be as favorable."

He renewed his struggle against the ropes. "What the holy *fuck* is going on!"

Lynn's eyes were soft, and a little misty. She looked as though she wanted to hold him, comfort him. But her voice was stressed, almost hard, when she spoke. "I can't tell you. Not now. But I assure you. If you pass, you will enjoy your existence here. Welcome to Earth."

* * *

No matter how many times Lynn read the data sheet, she couldn't make herself believe the results. What, exactly, were the odds that she would fall head over heels in love with a man as sterile as she was?

She groaned aloud, hiding her face in her hands. It couldn't be that he simply wasn't predisposed to fathering male children. Nope, he had the motility of an androgynous frog.

She shoved the paperwork across her desktop, stood, and paced her quarters. Once she turned her report over to her superiors, she and Camion might as well pick out adjoining burial plots.

Of course, if she could get them off the base – get them into the free zone – then it wouldn't matter. The rebels lived a hard life. They had few resources and lived outside the law. They were hunted by the government and only spent a few weeks at a time in one place. But it beat the hell out of a visit to the compression house.

She inhaled deeply, letting the infusion of canned oxygen silence her warring nerves.

What she needed was a plan. A fool-proof plan to break Camion out of the holding cell four security gates away, get them both off the base without being seen, commandeer a mode of transportation, locate the rebel forces that lurked just outside the confirmed borders of the United States, and bullshit their way into the free zone.

Simple.

Her forehead hit the desk. She was so fucked.

* * *

If Camion never saw another cage again in his life, it would be too soon. Cells had changed a bit in . . . holy fuck . . . a thousand years, but a cage was a cage. It didn't matter that there were no bars. Instead, an iridescent light swirled like smoke caught in a slice of sunlight through a bedroom curtain. As soon as Reese and three other women had tossed him, chained and pissed off, onto a cement bench, the lighted walls had appeared like magic. Then Reese had tossed a pencil into the light. It had fallen to the floor, sliced cleanly in two. The Light Defense, as she'd called it, wasn't magical. At least he hadn't completely lost his mind. No, the power source was plainly visible embedded in the floor.

Everywhere he looked in the holding facility backed up what Lynn had told him. He was most definitely in a future world. A map of the United States hung on the wall over a steel desk. At least, it was labeled as a map of the U.S. It looked like a map of the Intermountain West: Nevada, Utah, Idaho, Colorado, part of Wyoming, and northern New Mexico and Arizona. The map below it revealed something even more disheartening. Nevada made up the West Coast, and the rest of the North American continent had been labeled 'Rebel Territory' in thick, green letters.

What had happened to the world in the past thousand years? Were the people of his time responsible, or had something happened later to cause such a drastic downfall? He laid his head in his hands, inhaled a deep, cleansing breath then pulled his hair out of his face, fisting the strands at the back of his head. He blew out a loud breath.

The pregnant woman at the desk glanced in his direction. "Something wrong, Drake?"

Raising an eyebrow, he pushed himself to his feet. "You got a deck of cards or something?" She was cute. Bright golden hair, full mouth.

"Doubtful. This isn't a social club."

"No kidding. Really?"

She smiled, then pointed to her extended belly. "Sorry. I've been a bit cranky lately."

"Do you realize that just about every woman I've seen since they dragged me in here has been expecting?"

This time, she laughed. Leaning back in her chair, she patted her belly. "We're breeders. It's part of our job."

"Breeders? Job? This is too weird."

"Don't you know why you're here?"

"Honestly? I haven't the slightest clue."

"You must show promise in the little fishy department. They brought you back because you are predisposed to baring male children. Basically, we're out of boys."

For the next several minutes, Camion leaned against the bars with his arms folded across his chest while he listened to the guard explain the current state of affairs in the 29th Century. When she finished, she picked up her pen and turned her attention to her reports. "So, the very fact you're here means you tested well. Which is good. Because we'd have no use for you if you didn't. You'll probably be bred within a few weeks, and ten months later, we'll see if the tests were accurate."

He straightened and pushed himself off the bars. "What the hell does that mean?"

"We'll see if you produce male offspring. Or not."

"And if I don't?"

The guard made a slashing motion across her neck and winked.

She was kidding, right?

Fuck or die? Christ. What kind of a freaked-out Amazon tribe had he stumbled into?

The door opened and Lynn strode through the opening like a general heading into battle. She'd pulled her hair back into a severe bun. Her uniform consisted of black slacks complete with creases he could cut his finger on, a khaki shirt with long sleeves, and a chest full of service ribbons. Her left sleeve bore three hashmarks, denoting twelve years of service – if the standards hadn't changed since his days in the SEALs. She wore one of those odd guns on her hip. The term 'Blaster' came to mind and he half-expected C3PO to waddle through the door behind her.

But, even with the sharp lines of her uniform and the stark, almost robotic, mannerisms . . . he still wanted her. Blood rushed to his cock the second she walked into the room.

She didn't acknowledge him; didn't even look at him. Instead, she focused her attention on the woman at the desk. He shouldn't have expected anything less. She was a Manhunter. He was a breeding stock.

Great. *Moo.*

But he'd hoped. The way she'd looked at him about the Holy Grail made him think the feelings and time they'd shared hadn't been for nothing.

Obviously, he'd been wrong.

"I have orders to remove the prisoner to Amazonia." Lynn handed a sheaf of papers to the pregnant guard.

"This is highly irregular. I was expecting the transportation team to take him at the end of the week after the other squads report back."

Lynn squared her shoulders. "I'm only following orders."

The guard sifted through the papers. When she reached one of the last sheets, her eyes widened. "No kidding?" she murmured.

"What you got there?" he asked, trying to sound nonchalant.

The guard handed the papers back to Lynn and stood, grabbing the keys to the power source from their hook as she rose. "You, Studly, have an appointment at the farm. Apparently, you're also predisposed to multiples."

"Whatever . . ." He shrugged.

"It means twins and triplets, bright one. They want to breed you right away. So, you have a ticket to Amazonia and a date with a Breeder."

"Oh. Joy."

The possibility of taking both women hostage and shooting his way out of his immediate surroundings crossed his mind, briefly. He dismissed it as easily as it came. If Lynn was his escort to wherever the hell they were sending him, he could escape once they hit the road and not risk the life of an expectant mother and her child. When the cell opened, he exited quietly and allowed Lynn to place the cuffs on his wrists.

Her fingertips brushed against his forearms, sending electricity straight to his prick. It leapt against his will and fired his blood while reminding him of the effect her touch had on not only his body, but his heart. She tugged hard on the cuffs to check their soundness. He winced.

She continued to ignore him, other than taking his bicep in a firm grip and shoving him toward the door. He didn't move. Instead, he glared down at the top of head. "Say please."

"Move," she growled. "I don't have time for your games."

He feigned a shocked expression. "She speaks."

Shoving him again, she pointed to the door.

Outside, they approached what could only be described as a gray truck – though it looked nothing like any truck he'd ever seen. Six wheels – two in the front, four in the back – and a scooped cattle guard mounted to the front denoted it as a hard-working machine. The roof had no less than three satellite receivers and the dash console looked like something out of Star Trek. But then, it would, wouldn't it? Lynn settled him in the rear seat and flipped a switch on the ceiling. A system of seatbelts wrapped around his waist and shoulders.

She circled the truck and slid behind the steering wheel. "Hang on to something, Drake. It's gonna be a bumpy ride."

He winced inwardly. Considering what those words had meant when they'd escaped to his old hideout, this couldn't be good.

CHAPTER SEVEN

Lynn mashed the gas pedal and directed the huge Landcraft XG-17 to the first set of security gates. This one would be easy. As they approached, the guard tucked a lock of hair behind her ear, peered into the cab, and waved them through.

Camion's thick, warm voice came from the back. "You hold any tighter to that wheel and you're going to cut off the circulation to your fingers."

"Just be quiet. I'm concentrating."

"Concentrating on what, exactly? You're just doing your job, right?"

"Shut up!"

The quick glance she stole into the video monitor embedded in the dashboard proved they weren't followed. Yet. But it was still early.

The second gate brought her to a complete stop

while the guards used long-handled mirrors to inspect the undercarriage. They checked her paperwork.

"Breathe," Camion urged. His voice was barely above a whisper. Conspiratorial at the very least.

She spun to the back seat. His handsome face stalled her heartbeat for more than a second, and the half-smile he wore exposed a dimple she hadn't noticed before. "What?"

"Breathe. You're not breathing."

She took a deep breath. "Yes, I am. Hush."

"Thanks, Lieutenant. Carry on." The guard returned the forged papers and signaled her partner to open the gate.

Two down. Two to go.

They made it through the third gate with no problem, either. Thank God.

The fourth, and final, gate – the one that separated them from the civilian world and the beginnings of freedom – loomed in front of her like a giant predator with gaping jaws. Go through and there was no coming back.

The paperwork she'd created last night had fooled three sets of guards. But it wouldn't fool the Marines who took their duties as the last sentinels of the Top Secret establishment very seriously. She pulled to the side of the road and threw the Landcraft into neutral. She scanned the Light Defense system in both directions. The bluish-green light swirled like an oil spill on the ocean all along the fence line. The power source that provided the decapitating force was buried in the earth every one-point-five meters around the entire installation. It didn't matter that the sources were too close together to allow a vehicle to pass between them. If they were on, the lightforce would destroy anything that touched it.

There was nothing left to do but wait, and pray that her brother would do his part before the guards got suspicious and came to see why the hell she was sitting on the side of the road like a lump.

"Is there a problem?" Camion's voice washed over her like a slow, meandering wave. Like the tides, he pulled on her soul.

"No," she choked. "Everything's fine."

A figure appeared on the roof of the watchtower. Her brother, the last male born in their time, waved his subproclear power rifle over his head.

Now, or never.

After she pulled back on the roadway, she increased speed. The closer she came to the huge, black outpost, the faster she pushed the twin engines.

Two of the guards stepped into the street, but she didn't slow down. She shifted into the next gear.

"What the fuck are you doing?" Camion yelled from the back.

"Figure it out!" She stomped harder on the reactor pedal and threw the engine into the highest gear.

The guards scrambled and dashed out of the way at the last possible minute. A second before the Landcraft hit the Lightforce gates at seventy-nine kilometers per hour, the swirling color vanished.

Ahead of them, the empty space of Western Colorado's New Sahara Desert spread out like a sheet of nothing.

A second later, Camion's face appeared next to her. He crawled over the seat awkwardly, his hands still fastened behind his back.

"How did you get loose?"

"I'm full of surprises. Just drive." He twisted in the seat to look out the back window. "Yup. They're pissed."

Lynn stole a glance at the monitor. One of the guards raised his subproclear rifle in their direction. Her brother did, as well. But she wasn't worried about him. He'd miss, for sure. The first soldier released a blast of light energy, bright red and gaining on them fast. Lynn engaged the deflection shields.

"What did you just do?" Camion asked, studying the console.

"Shields. You know, like in Star Wars?"

"Cool."

A blast of energy hit the craft. Ineffective except for a slight stutter in the engine, it bounced off the shield with a stunning light display.

"You got keys for these things?" Camion motioned to his handcuffs.

"In my pocket."

Camion turned his back to her, shifted on the seat and maneuvered his long fingers into her front pocket. Heat stole into her cheeks at the contact until he found the keys and withdrew them. A moment later, he was free.

"So what's our next move, Cochise?"

"Cochise?"

"Nevermind. What's your plan?"

"Well, we should have enough power to get us to Little Vegas. We can hide out there for a couple of days."

"Sounds promising. The shacking up part. And then?"

"I have no idea."

* * *

Lynn slept. Curled into a tiny ball in the center of a huge bed at the Nebular Hotel and Casino, she looked like a kitten – all fur and claws but no real fight. That wasn't true. She'd fought. She'd fought for him.

When they'd checked into the hotel – using a strange substance that he assumed was a drug of some kind instead of the debit-type card everyone else used – he'd had one thing on his mind. Paying her back for her little medical experiment on board ship.

They'd been in the room long enough to drop her single piece of luggage and shut the door before he'd pushed her against the wall. He'd used one hand to hold her arms above her head, and the other to strip her of her uniform. Within seconds, she'd been naked, his jeans had been around his knees, and he'd been fucking her against the wall like a man possessed.

His stomach clenched at the memory of her hands on his body. The way she'd thrust her hips against him, grinding and humping as though she were as desperate as he.

Afterward, she'd looked so tired, he'd insisted she take a shower and get some rest. She'd sauntered into the bathroom, her bare ass reflecting the slivers of light that poured through the draperies on the other side of the room.

Her nap afforded him the time he needed to scope out his surroundings, acclimate to his new environment – and search the overnight bag she'd conveniently pulled from the back of the truck.

The environment had been easy. Vegas never

changed, no matter what state it was in now. He'd checked out the casino, quenched his thirst in the bar, and noted the incredible number of women who played the tables or tended bar. As far as he could tell from the curious, appreciative glances he'd received everywhere he went – he was just about the only man in the joint. Except for the occasional naked dancer who bumped and ground on platforms spotted throughout the casino floor.

The surroundings proved to be a fairly typical urban city. Life carried on like usual outside the casino. Women in scanty clothing and spiked heels plied their trade on the street corners, obviously picking up other women. Given his gender, he didn't stay outside very long. He stuck out like a sore . . . thumb.

Now, he sat at a small, circular table in their room in front of the huge, plate-glass windows overlooking the strip. Rather, the 'new' strip. A cold beer within easy reach, he rummaged through

Lynn's bag. Clothing. Toiletries. An electronic device about the size of an MP3 player, but with a fold-out screen. Ebook reader, maybe?

At the bottom of the bag, he found a sheath of papers that looked a lot like the one she'd been showing the various guards. He picked up his beer and started reading.

The report detailed Lynn's experiences in the 21st Century. Words like 'failed to perform' and 'dereliction of duty' raised his eyebrows. Turning the page, he found a copy of something called a Virility Report.

He noticed his name on the page, then one word caught his attention. Sterile.

He frowned, shifting in his chair. He wasn't sterile. Virile, yes. Shooting blanks? C'mon!

He turned to the last page. Then dropped his beer.

Summons for Execution.

The official-looking, legal document bore his

name, and Lynn's. His name was typed in the To Be Executed field. Hers was in the Sanctioned by field.

"I couldn't go through with it." The strained voice came from behind him. Sleepy and just husky enough to make his dick jump, Lynn seemed to struggle against tears.

Still, he couldn't make himself turn around. He couldn't face her. "You were going to have me murdered."

"No," she raised her voice. The sound of squeaking springs and then a heavy footfall echoed in the hollows of his mind while she scrambled off the bed. "No, I wasn't. I did my reports; I put the information into the computer. Those papers are printed automatically. When I read them, when I saw what that information meant . . ." Suddenly, she was on her knees beside his chair, pulling at his arm in an effort to gain his complete attention.

He finally faced her. Her expression was drawn and tired, but beautiful. The blue of her eyes shone with unshed tears. Her lips trembled.

"Don't you understand? When I read the final report, I couldn't allow it to happen. I love you, Camion. Can't you see that?"

"If they find you, they'll kill you, won't they?"

She nodded, casting her gaze to the floor.

Taking her jaw with the tip of one finger, he raised her face. "I won't let that happen."

"I believe you."

Rising slowly, Camion drew her with him. The loose tee-shirt she'd worn to bed hung off one shoulder, revealing the creamy flesh beneath. She'd scrubbed her face clean of all traces of makeup when she'd showered and her skin practically glowed. Her lips parted. She brushed her tongue over them, leaving a tempting shimmer.

He led her to the bed, gently urging her down while he lifted her shirt over her head. Naked, she reclined on the rumpled sheets. His pulse raced at the sight of her supine body, welcoming him.

She was so different from the woman he'd met at the bar. Was it only yesterday? He couldn't imagine how she'd incorporated herself into his existence in such a short time, but he didn't care. She belonged to him. The overwhelming possessiveness was as much a part of him as his hands.

Or his heart.

He stripped out of his jeans, dropping them where they fell. When he joined her on the bed, she reached for him, but he stopped her. Holding her wrists in both hands, he pinned them above her head. "Let's get one thing clear, right from the beginning. From now on, I'm in charge."

She giggled. "We'll see-"

He cut off her response with a kiss. She tasted sweet, like she was made of candy. Moving his lips against hers seemed as natural as breathing or thinking. Though, if he had to admit it, he found rational thought impossible where she was concerned.

Tiny moans escaped her when he left her mouth and moved to her breasts. He nipped and suckled first one, then the other while he held her wrists firmly in place.

This time he would make love to her slowly. This time, he would savor whatever it was that drove him to consume her – whatever it was that made him feel whole and complete whenever they were together.

Lynn shifted her hips against his thigh. Spreading her legs, she purred, "Touch me, Camion."

Her cleft was smooth, like silk. Moist heat surrounded his finger as he drew it from her center and over her swollen nub. He lingered there for more than a breath, savoring the feel of it against his finger. Sliding downward, he traced kisses over her torso. She responded to his touch as nobody ever had before. It was as if her desire drove him, enhancing every pulse of wicked greed that fed his growing desire for her.

Positioning himself over her cleft, he dropped his mouth to suckle her clitoris. Immediately, she thrust her hips against his lips – begging for more without saying a word.

Lynn felt like the world was hers to command. At the same time, her bones turned to mush and her stomach did back-flips every time Camion stroked her clitoris so masterfully, it took her breath away. His tongue tasted and teased her to heights she'd never realized were possible. "More," she panted. "More."

The bed dipped beneath his weight. Slowly, like a predator, he climbed her. Soft tickles of delight spread like feathered wings over her flesh. He captured her mouth in a deep, probing kiss. He tasted of her, as though she'd branded him. When the probing tip of his cock brushed against her crotch, a gasp formed in her throat. Hungry for something only he could fulfill, she arched her body into him. He groaned. She shivered.

Slowly, he entered her. His thrusts were sure and strong. Possessive. Powerful. Beneath her fingers, his back muscles dipped and swayed. Molten fire thundered through her veins with each lunge of his hips.

Wings of angels bore her passion to a rapturous pinnacle, higher and higher. Until, too quickly, the universe exploded around her and sent her careening in a million directions at once.

A moment later, Camion thrust once, twice . . . then stilled as his cock throbbed within her innermost folds. "Lynn," he whispered.

He fell against her, his weight a delightful and gentle caress. When their breathing returned to normal, he placed a slow, heavy kiss in the crook of her neck and rolled away. "You're trying to kill me, after all," he quipped.

He opened his arms. As though they'd spent an eternity reading each other's minds, she slid next to him and laid her head on his shoulder.

Unavoidably, the world fell back into place. Lynn tried not to shudder, but when her body trembled, Camion held her closer. "I'm not trying to kill you," she replied, smiling. "But we do have to get out of here. Soon."

He kissed the top of her head. "What do we do now?"

"We'll go to the free zone."

"Sure."

"It's outside the borders of the U.S. The government doesn't care about the people there. They're called rebels, but that's just a name, really. Because they haven't conformed, they can't exist inside the borders. They have no way to survive. There's just one thing."

"What's that?"

"Until we convince them we're legit, *they'll* probably try to kill us."

He laughed. "So what else is new?" Then he

wrapped his arms around her, and pulled her naked, pliant body against his chest. She drew haphazard shapes on his chest. "It doesn't matter. They can try. I'm not so easy to kill, Lynn, in case you haven't noticed. We'll get through it. Together."

The End

Did you enjoy reading *Hunting Camion*

by Raleigh Kincaid?

Please leave a short review on your favorite online book site! Independent authors count on your reviews to help them succeed. You can write to the author directly at the following website: www.marjoriejones.info

About the Author

When Marjorie Jones wants to write something a little on the steamy side, she calls upon her old friend, Raleigh Kincaid. Named for one of her favorite cities near her East Coast roots and a love of all things Scottish, Raleigh is the fire cracker

Marjorie wishes she could be.

Raleigh, Marjorie and their wife live in Utah with their shared children, numbering somewhere between six and ten and ranging in age from I-promise-I-don' to the-best-dad-in-the-history-of-the-world.

MORE GREAT BOOKS FROM MARJORIE JONES!

<u>*Look for these other titles by Marjorie Jones*</u>
- Loving the Heartland (Indie Artist Press)
- The Jewel and the Sword (Medallion Press)
- My Lady's Will (Champagne Books)
- The Lighthorseman (Medallion Press)
- The Flyer (Medallion Press)
- Hope (Indie Artist Press)
- A Love for All Time (Indie Artist Press, Writing as Raleigh Kincaid)
- Firelight (Indie Artist Press, Writing as Starla Childs)
- Dance in My Heart (Indie Artist Press)
- Dawn of Love (Champagne Books, Writing as Starla Childs)
- Dawn of Redemption (Champagne Books, Writing as Starla Childs)

Please enjoy this peek into

A Love For All Time,

a novella from Raleigh Kincaid

A smile brushed her lips and she hurried to their secret meeting place.

She was surprised to find Percicus already there. With his back facing her, she appreciated the solid muscles that rippled beneath bronzed flesh. He'd removed his linen tunic and draped it over the stone bench next to a cistern. Cupping his hands, he dipped them in the water, filled them, then tossed the water over his bare shoulders. He bathed quickly, finishing with a few splashes of water over his long, ebony hair. Droplets glistened like diamonds while he moved with the grace of a cat; liquid and a little mysterious. The droplets ran in haphazard rivulets until they met the waistband of his leggings, set low on his narrow hips. When he heard her approach, he turned in her direction and his full, soft lips spread into a welcoming smile.

She adored his smile. It was wide and genuine. He didn't look at her as if she were any less valuable than he was. The fact he didn't care she was merely a handmaiden, born of lowly circumstances and not fit to love him, shone in the appreciative glances he'd passed her since the day they'd met. That day, six years before, when she'd been selected to tend his mother.

Happiness cascaded over her flesh with tiny kisses, raising bumps of anticipation. Percicus loved her. And she loved him.

"I feared I wouldn't be able to get away," he explained. "So I invented an excuse before my father could find some other political rant with which to trap the council for another half-day."

He took her in his arms, pressing his lips against hers in what might have been a chaste kiss. Except, it changed almost as soon as they touched. The fire that burned between them leapt and danced at the first hint of contact. Her body turned from flesh and bone to uncut wine in a matter of seconds. Percicus' hands found their way down her back, tracing an inferno over her spine, until they cupped her bottom and pulled her hips against the raging heat of his shaft.

Only two thin layers of summer linen separated their bodies from the waist down. Only one barred her breasts from joining with the muscles of his chest. On the far side of the bench, a soft field of cultured grass lay empty in the shadow of the temple. He led her there, and eliminated the barriers between them.

Lying naked on the fragrant earth, she watched him remove the last of his clothing. He had to have been born of the gods. No mortal man could be so perfect. Smooth skin reflected the beams of sunlight that splintered through the columns of the temple. His waist was narrow, his hips as well. He wore the body of a warrior lord easily, as he should. Long, lean and powerful enough to love her, even though it could cost them both their lives.

But that didn't matter when he knelt at her feet, took her right ankle in his battle-roughened hands and gently placed a kiss in the small, tender recess just behind the bone. From there, he trailed his lips over the inside of her calf, pausing at her knee to administer to the soft flesh at the back. Finally, he reached the sensitive area inside her thigh. He languished there not at all before placing his mouth over the very center of her soul. That part of her that he knew would delight in his attentions until the floodgates of passion took her to another level of existence.

www.ingramcontent.com/pod-product-compliance
Lightning Source LLC
Chambersburg PA
CBHW030414120726
47904CB00007B/2276